DATE			

A NOTE TO PARENTS

When your children are ready to "step into reading," giving them the right books—and lots of them—is as crucial as giving them the right food to eat. **Step into Reading Books** present exciting stories and information reinforced with lively, colorful illustrations that make learning to read fun, satisfying, and worthwhile. They are priced so that acquiring an entire library of them is affordable. And they are beginning readers with an important difference—they're written on four levels.

Step 1 Books, with their very large type and extremely simple vocabulary, have been created for the very youngest readers. **Step 2 Books** are both longer and slightly more difficult. **Step 3 Books,** written to mid-second-grade reading levels, are for the child who has acquired even greater reading skills. **Step 4 Books** offer exciting nonfiction for the increasingly proficient reader.

Children develop at different ages. **Step into Reading Books,** with their four levels of reading, are designed to help children become good—and interested—readers *faster*. The grade levels assigned to the four steps—preschool through grade 1 for Step 1, grades 1 through 3 for Step 2, grades 2 and 3 for Step 3, and grades 2 through 4 for Step 4—are intended only as guides. Some children move through all four steps very rapidly; others climb the steps over a period of several years. These books will help your child "step into reading" in style!

Text copyright © 1973 by Lynn Hall. Illustrations copyright © 1992 by Antonio Castro.
All rights reserved under International and Pan-American Copyright Conventions. Published in the
United States by Random House, Inc., New York, and simultaneously in Canada by Random House
of Canada Limited, Toronto. Originally published in different form by Touchwood Press in 1973.

Library of Congress Cataloging-in-Publication Data
Hall, Lynn.
  Barry, the bravest Saint Bernard / by Lynn Hall ; illustrated by Antonio Castro.
    p.   cm. – (Step into reading. A step 4 book)
  Summary: Relates the feats of Barry, the Saint Bernard dog whose name, to this day, honors the
best dog at the Saint Bernard Monastery.
  ISBN 0-679-83054-5 (pbk.)   ISBN 0-679-93054-X (lib. bdg.)
  1. Barry (Dog)–Juvenile literature.   2. Saint Bernard dog–Switzerland–Biography–Juvenile
literature.   3. Rescue dogs–Switzerland–Biography–Juvenile literature.   [1. Barry (Dog)   2.
Saint Bernard dog.   3. Dogs.]   I. Castro, Antonio, ill.   II. Title.   III. Series: Step into reading.
Step 4 book. SF 429.S3H35   1992   636.7′3–dc20   92-1228

Manufactured in the United States of America   10 9 8 7 6 5 4

STEP INTO READING is a trademark of Random House, Inc.

Step into Reading

BARRY
The Bravest
Saint Bernard

By Lynn Hall
Illustrated by Antonio Castro

A Step 4 Book

Random House 🏠 New York

The snow in the mountain pass was pink from the setting sun. Even the walls and windows of the stone buildings looked pink.

Werner stepped out of the monastery kitchen into the deep snow. In his arms he carried a huge tub of dog food. He pulled back the heavy door of the dogs' building.

"Dinner time!" he called.

The room inside was big and almost bare. There were piles of straw against the walls. Now, from the straw came huge brown and white dogs. There were fourteen of them, and even the smallest was heavier than Werner.

"Don't push, now," Werner said. "You'll all get your supper."

The dogs pressed close, but they were gentle. They seemed to know how strong they were. Werner filled each of their dishes. Then he took the last dish, the biggest one, to a quiet corner of the room.

One of the dogs left the others and followed him.

"There you are, Barry. I saved the best for you." Werner stood close to the giant animal.

Before he began eating, Barry pushed

his head up under Werner's chin and snuffled. He took the boy's arm in his huge jaws and shook it. Werner laughed. Barry growled and shook it harder, as he always did.

The Saint Bernard Monastery, where the dogs lived, was high in the mountains of Switzerland. In those days there were no cars or highways, only horses and mountain trails. The only way over the mountains was through a long valley called the Saint Bernard pass.

The pass was named for the monastery, a huge stone building where monks lived and worked. The monks, who were very holy men, had a special kind of work to do. They helped travelers going through the pass. In winter the snow was deep and dangerous, and sometimes people were buried under huge snow slides, or avalanches. Then the monks tried to find them and save them.

For this special work, the monks of the Saint Bernard Monastery had bred a wonderful kind of dog, which was also called a Saint Bernard. The dogs were big and powerful and could smell people trapped under the snow.

Werner loved all of the dogs at the monastery, but there was a special love between him and Barry. And Barry, like Werner, was too young to help with the rescue work.

"It's too dangerous out there," the monks told Werner. "You and Barry will have to wait until you're older."

The boy and the dog played roughly for a few minutes. Then Werner picked up the tub and started back toward the warm, bright monastery kitchen. His own supper would be ready by now. He was hungry for it.

But Father Benedict called to him. "Werner, come here, please."

Father Benedict was standing beside two steaming horses. The men who had been riding the horses stood nearby.

Werner put down the tub and walked toward them. Father Benedict said, "We have guests, Werner. Will you take their horses, please?"

Werner smiled at the two men. He took their horses into the stable to make them comfortable for the night. As he pulled the saddle off one horse, the saddle bags hit his arm. They were very heavy. Werner hung the saddle on the side of the stall. Then he lit a candle and opened one of the bags.

He thought, "If I were a monk, I couldn't snoop like this. I'm glad I'm not one, yet."

Inside the bag were a heavy pistol and a leather sack. From the shape of the sack, Werner was sure it was full of coins. His heart began to pound with fear.

The door blew open. Werner jumped. But it was only Father Benedict.

"Come here, Father," he called softly. He would have to admit that he had snooped. But that was better than being shot by robbers.

Father Benedict came into the stall.

"Look," Werner said. "Those men are thieves! There's a gun in this bag, and a sack of gold. I know I shouldn't have looked, but..."

Father Benedict spoke calmly. "The doors of Saint Bernard are open to anyone who needs shelter."

"But, Father! They have a gun. They came to rob us."

The monk just smiled. He said, "We don't know that, do we? One of our guests asked for his bags. I'll take them. You go on inside before your supper gets cold." The monk took the saddle bags. He calmly slipped them over his arm.

As Werner walked toward the lighted kitchen, he shook his head. Father Benedict's unfailing calm often puzzled the boy. The Father followed Werner into the kitchen.

The large warm kitchen smelled of soup and onions. At the long table sat twelve monks and the two travelers. Werner sat at the far end, away from the strangers. He tried to see their faces, but it was impossible. Six robed monks sat in between them.

When the meal was finally over, one of the strangers stood up. In his hand was the gun!

"I thank you for the food," he said. "Now I'll thank you for your money."

Fearfully Werner looked at the gun. Then he looked at the monks across from him. Their faces were calm.

Father Benedict spoke. "We are a poor order. We have no money."

The robber laughed. "I know better than that. Everyone stand up and stay close together."

The monks and Werner got up from the table. They moved to the middle of the room. It seemed to Werner that he was the only one who was afraid.

Father Benedict said, "Very well. I see I can't fool you. Come this way."

He opened the door and went out into the yard. The monks, with Werner in the center, walked behind. The robbers followed the monks. With great dignity, Father Benedict moved toward the dogs' building. Werner was confused. There was no treasure in there, he knew. He opened his mouth to speak. The monk

beside him poked him with his elbow.

At the door Father Benedict stopped. He stood aside. "All of our wealth is behind these doors," he said. "Gentlemen, help yourselves!"

The robbers ran forward. They pulled at the heavy doors. The doors opened, and fourteen huge animals leaped out. Their mouths were open. Their teeth shone in the moonlight. The biggest one grabbed a robber's arm. He shook it and began to growl.

The robbers screamed as the dogs knocked the gun loose. The gun flew through the air. It landed softly in the snow. Still screaming, the men ran into the stable. A few seconds later, they came out riding their horses bareback. They disappeared into the darkness.

The monks laughed and went back to the bright, warm kitchen. Werner led the dogs into their building. He was grinning.

"Barry, you old robber-chaser, you really scared them. And I'm so glad!"

The dog growled and gently took Werner's wrist in his mouth. His tail wagged with happiness.

The months passed, and soon summer came.

The mountains were so high that even in summer it snowed nearly every week, but the snow melted almost as it fell. Flowers bloomed with snow on their petals. The mountains were beautiful in summer.

Barry had his first birthday in June, and his training began. Brother Luigi, the

elderly trainer, took Barry and the other young dogs out every morning. They romped in the snow for three hours. Werner went along to watch and learn, and help when he could. Brother Luigi would soon be too old to handle the big dogs. Werner hoped to take his place someday.

Werner's part in the training was to hide from the dogs. He would bury himself in the snow. Then he'd wait until one of the dogs found him and dug him up. All of the dogs were experts at smelling a human through the snow, but Barry's big nose seemed more remarkable than the others'. Almost always, it was Barry who found Werner first. The huge dog would dig away the snow. Then he would put his warm body close to Werner's and lick the boy's face. They both pretended Werner was freezing to death. Werner lay as still as he could while Barry's tongue tickled him. When he could stand it no longer, he began to giggle. Then Barry's tail wagged with joy. They rolled together in the snow.

When winter came, Barry was allowed to go on real journeys along the pass. He helped guide travelers and looked for people who might be in trouble. An avalanche could quickly bury anyone in its path. If help didn't arrive in time, the

victims would freeze or smother from lack of air.

Every morning Barry went down the mountain with Luigi or one of the other monks. There, beside the trail, was a stone hut. If there were travelers waiting in the hut, the dogs led them up the trail through the dangerous mountain pass. It was an all-day walk.

By the end of that winter, it was clear that Barry was the best rescue dog the monks had ever had. When an avalanche struck, Barry was the first to find people buried under the snow. He was the fastest to dig them out. Barry worked hardest to warm them up. Sometimes the other dogs gave up. But Barry would go on licking a frozen face until there was some movement. Then the great dog would go wild with joy.

Years passed. Werner grew tall and thin. Now he gave all of his time to the dogs. He worked with Brother Luigi every day. He fed the dogs, played with them, and helped train the pups. He was completely happy.

When Barry was six years old, Werner was eighteen. That was the most terrible winter the monks had known. Rescue trips were made every day. Half of the monastery dogs died that winter, trying to save the travelers' lives. Many of the monks died, too, lost in blizzards from which their own brave dogs could not save them.

One night in late March, Werner and Barry were walking slowly up the trail toward home. Werner's face was stiff with cold. Even Barry seemed tired. It had been a terrible winter for both of them.

The sky was black. The mountain peaks, so close on either side, could not be seen in the dark. Only a faint glow rose from the snow.

Suddenly there was a roar above them, like thunder. Werner and Barry both knew the sound, and dreaded it. Werner got down on his knees and pulled Barry close to him. The roar became a

SWOOSH. A wall of snow came down the mountainside, just behind them.

When the night was still again, Werner got up. His heart was pounding.

"That was too close, Barry," he said. "We were almost killed. Let's get home and let them know we're all right."

He walked on, but Barry did not follow. The dog stood looking up the mountainside. He was sniffing the air.

"Is there someone up there? Go and find him."

The dog came to him, one slow step at a time. When he got to Werner, his tail moved slowly from side to side.

Werner reached for the bundle on the dog's back.

"Father Benedict!" Werner shouted as loudly as he could. The call echoed back from the mountain peaks. "Benedict…dict …dict.…"

A woman's shawl was tied around Barry's chest. Under the shawl Werner's hands found a child. It was a small boy whose body was stiff.

From the monastery Father Benedict and the others came running. Their black robes rose like wings behind them. They breathed into the boy's mouth. They rubbed him with snow to make his blood move faster through his body. He moved, cried out.

While the monks worked on the nearly frozen child, Werner led Barry into the dogs' building. Gently he fed Barry. The great dog was so tired he could barely chew. When he stretched out on the straw to sleep, his head was in Werner's lap. His jaws gently held Werner's arm.

It was several days before the body of the child's mother was found. When Barry had found her and her son, she was very weak. She was just able to tie the boy onto Barry's back with her shawl before she died.

After that rescue, Barry's fame spread all over the world. In England, a thirteen-year-old boy drew a picture of Barry from the stories he had heard of the rescue. That boy grew up to be Sir Edwin Landseer, a famous painter of dogs.

Three years later, Brother Luigi was lost during a rescue trip. When the old trainer did not come home, Father Benedict opened the kennel door and told Barry, "Find your master."

Barry found him, buried under tons of snow. The great dog worked harder than he had ever worked before, but it was too late. Luigi was dead. Sadly, Werner took over the trainer's duties.

Three years passed. It was October, and the day had been crisply cool. But as night came, the first heavy snow of the year began to fall.

In the kitchen of the monastery, three old friends sat enjoying the fire and the company of one another. Father Benedict and Werner sat close to the fireplace. Barry lay nearby, between the two men. He didn't like the heat from the fire, but he hated to be more than a few feet from Werner.

Werner had become a monk, and he was now a young man of twenty-four. He moved his foot and rubbed the toe of his shoe against Barry's hip. The dog's eyes stayed closed, but his tail thumped the floor. He rolled over onto his back so Werner's foot could rub under his ribs.

The dark spots on Barry's head now showed some white hairs. His back sagged slightly with age when he walked. But

when the monastery dogs were let out each morning for their run in the snow, Barry still bounded with them through the blue-white drifts.

It had been still in the kitchen for several minutes when Werner said, "I'm being selfish, am I not?"

The two men were such close friends that Father Benedict didn't need to ask what Werner meant.

"It isn't easy to give up a friend like Barry," the Father said gently.

"Still, this must be his last year," Werner said. "The winters are too cold up here for an old dog. I think we may not use him this winter for rescue work. We'll let him stay here, just for company. Then next summer, when we take the puppies down to the city to be sold, Barry can go along. Our friends will keep him there, and he can rest in a warmer place. He has earned that."

The Father smiled down at the sleeping dog. "Yes, Barry has been the greatest of all our dogs. There may never be another rescue dog who works with the devotion of this old fellow. Barry has saved forty lives all by himself. It is indeed a fine record."

"I hope this summer's pups will—" Werner was interrupted by the sound of the knocker at the front door. He and the Father exchanged glances—it was late for travelers. The two men moved through the long stone hallway. The yawning, wagging Barry followed them sleepily.

Werner pulled open the huge doors. He saw a shivering boy standing on the steps.

"Come inside," he said.

The boy was taken quickly to the kitchen. Because his hands were so stiff with cold, Werner helped him take off his coat. The monks stirred up the fire in the stove and set a pot of soup on to boil.

When the boy was able to talk, he said, "I thank you for your kindness." He was small and thin. His clothes were those of a farmer's son.

He went on. "My brother Martin ran away from home three days ago. He was called to serve in the army, and didn't want to go. So he ran away. He took only his jacket, a loaf of bread, and a knife to cut it with. Our mother told me to come and ask you to look for him." The boy's eyes were shining with tears which he tried to hide.

Father Benedict said, "Do you know which way he went?"

Werner had already left to call the other monks and wake up the dogs.

Within minutes the search party was on its way—eight monks and six dogs. Werner had shut Barry in the kitchen, but before the party had reached the trail, the old dog found an open door. He raced to join Werner.

A full moon lighted the night. The snow had stopped falling. Trees, rocks,

monks, and dogs were black against the pale gray snow. The group moved down the mountainside to a place the boy had named. Then they separated, monks and dogs spreading out to cover the area. Each monk carried a long stick to poke into the snow in case an avalanche had buried young Martin.

Barry and Werner moved lower on the mountain slope than the others. Most of Werner's mind was on the job of finding Martin. A part of it was thinking that this would probably be the last time he followed Barry's bushy tail through the mountains they both loved.

There had been hundreds of dogs in Werner's care these past years. Many were Barry's sons and daughters. All were fine dogs; each was lovable in his own way. But none had the deep wisdom that shone in Barry's eyes. None could equal the great old dog's ability to do his job of saving human lives. No other dog had ever meant so much to Werner.

The two of them were alone on the mountain slope. Barry moved ahead, his nose near the snow.

Suddenly he stopped. He raised his huge head and swung it slowly from side to side. Then he galloped down the hillside and disappeared behind a clump of pine trees. Werner called to the others and started after Barry.

Suddenly there was a scream. "Aaiii… BEAR!"

Werner rounded the trees and stopped. A young man held tightly to a tree. His eyes were wide and staring. In his hand was a knife, red with blood. At his feet lay Barry.

For the first time in his life, Werner paid no attention to the human. He knelt over Barry, and he wept. The dog's side and neck were laced with stab wounds.

But beneath the blood, the great heart beat on.

An hour later both Barry and Martin had been carried on stretchers to the monastery. The boy was asleep in the warmest of the guest rooms, with his young brother watching over him.

Barry lay on a bed of soft blankets near the kitchen fire while Werner cleaned and bandaged his wounds. The dog made no move. Around him stood a ring of silent black-robed men whose love for him shone in the wetness of their eyes.

"He's a very old dog," the Father said softly. "To lose that much blood..."

"He will get well." Werner's jaw was shut so hard the words could barely get out.

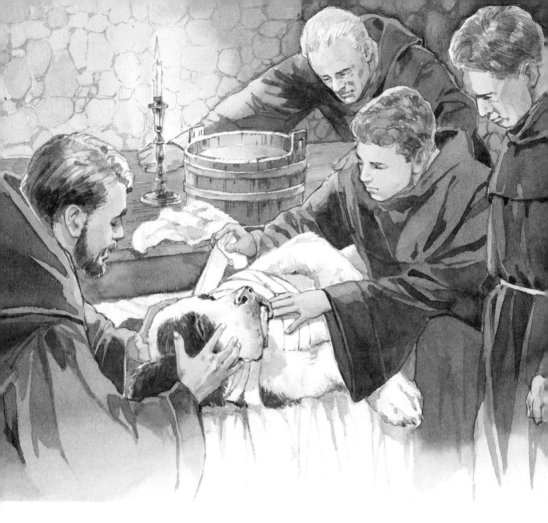

The Father put a hand on Werner's shoulder. "I hope you don't blame the boy. He was out of his head with cold and fear. Barry came leaping toward him in the moonlight. It was natural enough that he should mistake Barry for a bear. The lad was probably afraid of wild animals anyway."

Two years later, after a peaceful retirement in the village, Barry died of old age. His body was mounted and is now on display in a Swiss museum.

It was a hundred years after his death before the Saint Bernard monks had another dog great enough to be named Barry. Since that time it has become traditional to give the honored name of Barry to the finest dog at the monastery.

There is a Barry there today.